YUCKETYPOO

THE MONSTER THAT GREW AND GREW

LOLLYPOP PUBLISHING LTD

Registered in England
Registered Number 4712406
Registered Office - 4 Halesowen Street,
Rowley Regis, West Midlands B65 0HG

Published by Lollypop Publishing Ltd.
www.lollypoppublishing.co.uk

British Library Cataloguing in Publication Data
Manufactured in the United Kingdom.

ISBN Number 978-1-906788-03-2

YUCKETYPOO

THE MONSTER THAT GREW AND GREW

WRITTEN BY
JILLY HENDERSON-LONG

ILLUSTRATED
BY ASHLEY STEVENS

Published by
Lollypop Publishing Ltd.

YUCKETYPOO

CONTENTS

Page

YUCKETYPOO

CONTENTS CONTINUED

Page

For Olivia Grace Waters

With Love
xxx

YUCKETYPOO

IT BEGINS (The Sweet Wrapper)

Careless Annie in the street
dropped the wrapper from her sweet,
a gust of wind then swept the ground,
blew that wrapper round and round,
blew that wrapper left and right,
half the day and through the night,
blew that wrapper in the air,
until a 'something' saw it there,

If only Careless Annie knew,
how the monster
grew and grew.

YUCKETYPOO

THE CRISP PACKET

Messy Michael saw the bin,
wouldn't put his crisp pack in,
threw the crisp pack like a ball
over someone's garden wall.

Didn't see
so never knew
how the monster
grew and grew.

YUCKETYPOO

BROKEN GLASS

A dog on a walk cut open his paw,
went to the vet and barked at the door.
"My foot found some glass," the injured dog said.
"I'll fix it," said vet, "with my needle and thread."
The dog was so brave – as brave as can be,
but muttered "If only it hadn't cut me!"
"Don't worry," said vet, "your foot will get better.
Send me a cheque inside a letter!"
The dog hobbled home with a bit of a limp
as bold as he could (for he wasn't a wimp).
"In future," he moaned as he sat on the grass,
"I'll keep my eyes open for more broken glass!"

YUCKETYPOO

LEAFLET DROP

Lots of leaflets left around,
piling high upon the ground.

The problem is, as you'll agree,
they don't look nice to you and me.

Never mind, it's kind of nice,
they make good carpets for the mice!

YUCKETYPOO

THE COLA CAN

Who dropped the cola can
and left it in the street,

rolling in the wind,
kicked by running feet,

making such a clatter,
if only people knew,

something bad would find it.
The monster grew and grew.

YUCKETYPOO

THE LEFT BEHIND BROKEN TOYS

PART ONE   "THE BALL"

There once was a ball with a hole,
which had scored for its owner a goal.

But once the ball split,
they didn't want it,

so they whacked it away with a pole!

YUCKETYPOO

CHEWING GUM

Crunch chomp chew,
sticky like glue.
Bitey mighty minty.
Slurpy burpy chewy.

When it lost its flavour,
when it tired his jaw,
along came Messy Michael
who spat it on the floor!

Crunch chomp chew
sticking to your shoe.
Chewing gum for everyone.
The monster grew and grew.

YUCKETYPOO

RAT'S PICNIC

Rats in the sewer.
Rats in the street.
Rats in the litter bins,
finding stuff to eat.
Rats eating burgers.
Rats eating chips.
Rats eating everything
and licking their lips.
Rats having parties.
Rats having fun.
Rats having picnics
in the autumn sun.

YUCKETYPOO

THE POND – PART ONE

The fish in the pond were happy,
their pond was fresh and clean,
their human cleared it often,
it had a sparkly sheen.

The fish were always boasting
of how their pond was best,
such a lovely place to live, so bright,
so clean, so fresh.

But one day brought a mighty splash,
the fish were most perturbed.
What was that sinking in their pond?
They swam about, disturbed.
The Empress called a council,
they met below the lily,
all the fish were listening,
so frightened they felt silly!

"My friends," the Empress bubbled.
"We are in trouble here.
Something's sinking in our pond
and filling us with fear.
We have to check it out, and find out what is what.
I need some volunteers. How many have I got?"

(Turn to page 18)

9

YUCKETYPOO

OLD NEWSPAPERS

Watch them dancing down the lane,
drifting out and in,
papers people leave behind,
floating on the wind.
They weave between the motor cars
and hover on the breeze,
fluttering in the bushes
and waving from the trees,
flapping past the window,
and over hedges too.
But something really wanted them.
The monster grew and grew.

YUCKETYPOO

A TISSUE, DON'T BLESS YOU

Snotty
Spotty
Slimy
Sloppy
Squishie
Squashie
Soggy
Groggy
Yucky
Mucky
Pick-em-uppy
Germy tissues
Everywhere.

AAA- CHOOO!!!!

YUCKETYPOO

KYM'S BROKEN TOOTH

Kym's uncle paid a visit, took her to the zoo,
bought her lunch and lollipops,
bought her ice cream, too.
They looked at all the animals and
fed the farmyard friends,
Kym was having so much fun,
she hoped it wouldn't end.

They left the zoo at half past two,
and went to get the bus.
Kym said she was hungry and
kicked up quite a fuss.
Uncle took her down the road,
they went into a shop,
Uncle bought some lemonade
and Kym had Toffee Drops.

As they set off home again,
Kym chomped and chewed and bit,
then, munching on a Toffee Drop,
she broke her tooth on it!
She screamed and howled and hollered,
half the tooth had gone,
they went off to the dentist,
which wasn't any fun.

The dentist took the tooth out –
or what was left of it.
Kym had a great big gap now.
She even lisped a bit.
And as they left the dentist and
Uncle closed the door,
Kym decided there and then
that she'd eat sweets no more.

YUCKETYPOO

FORGOTTEN SANDWICH

"I don't want cheese!"
said Billy Smith.
"Cheese sandwiches aren't cool!
"I want some ham,"
said Billy Smith,
on his way to school.
He threw the sandwich
in the hedge,
he threw his apple, too.

I wonder what would find it?
The monster grew and grew.

YUCKETYPOO

THE LEFT BEHIND BROKEN TOYS

PART TWO "THE TEDDY"

There once was a teddy called Bean
whose owner was really quite mean.
When Bean lost her hair
and became a bald bear,
she was left by a dustbin in Keyne.

YUCKETYPOO

THE POORLY TREE

Lots of plastic shopping bags,
hanging from a tree,
caught up in its branches
for everyone to see.
This caused a tricky problem,
there was no room for leaves,
made the tree feel poorly,
it simply couldn't breathe.
"I hate these plastic shopping bags!"
the poorly tree declared.
"I look just like a circus clown
with funny coloured hair!"
Lots of children passed it
and shouted out with glee,
"Look at all the shopping bags
hanging in that tree!"

YUCKETYPOO

RUBBISH

Rubbish here.
Rubbish there.
Lots of rubbish
everywhere.

Nasty niffs.
Sickly whiffs.

What a pong.
What was wrong?

Rubbish brown.
Rubbish blue.

YUCKETYPOO

THE POND – PART TWO

You may recall from last time,
that something in their pond,
made the fish feel poorly.
They wondered what was wrong.
The Empress called a meeting,
and asked for volunteers
to see if they could find the thing
that filled them with such fear.

YUCKETYPOO

A wise old carp called Hi Lee,
raised a noble fin,
"I'll check it out, your highness,
I don't mind going in."
Another carp called Kelpy,
boldly flicked his tail.
"I'll help Hi Lee your highness,
I'm going in as well!"

The Empress was so grateful.
She thanked the noble carp.
"Our futures lie within your fins,"
she told them with great heart.
Just then, a little minnow,
panted into view.
"It's leaking now, your highness,
oh what are we to do?"

(Go to page 26)

YUCKETYPOO

THE HORRIBLE PONG

"Whatever is that dreadful smell?"
the people said one day,
pinching at their noses,
to keep the pong at bay.

No-one knew the answer.
The smell got really bad.
It made them feel quite queasy.
It made them all feel sad.

It had to be the sewers.
What a yucky poo.
The people put on gas masks.
The monster grew and grew.

YUCKETYPOO

THE VERY PROUD BUGGY

Once the stripy buggy
carried little bottoms,
comfortable and snuggy,
to the shops and to the park.
It proudly flashed its red and white
and boasted something rotten,
but really loved its children,
with all its buggy heart.
The babies grew (as babies do)
and once they went to school,
the buggy was forgotten
and left behind to stew.
Its handles fell to pieces,
and something ripped the seat.
The buggy got the hump as it
rusted in the street!

YUCKETYPOO

THE WISHFUL DUSTBIN

"I want to be a robot,"
a dustbin said one day.
"I want to be an aeroplane
and fly so far away!
I want to be a set of drums
and make a lot of row.
I want to be a flower pot.
I want to be a plough!"
"Why not be a dustbin,"
said a passing cat.
"No-one uses dustbins,
and that, my friend, is that!"

YUCKETYPOO

ABANDONED CAR

Dumped in a field,
forgotten and rusty,
leather seats stolen,
steering wheel dusty,
engine now gone and
tyres so shoddy.

Along came the monster.
It now had a body.

YUCKETYPOO

THE LEFT BEHIND BROKEN TOYS

PART THREE   "THE SCOOTER"

There once was a scooter so fine,
whose owner just grew all the time.
It looked bright and new,
all silver and blue,

but was dumped when its owner turned nine

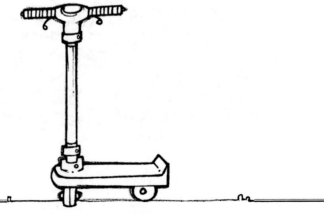

24

YUCKETYPOO

PLASTIC BOTTLES

Water bottles.
Pop bottles.
Milk bottles, too.

Bleach bottles.
Soap bottles.
Bottles for glue.

Big bottles.
Small bottles,
open and closed.

Along came the monster.
Now it had toes!

YUCKETYPOO

THE POND – PART THREE

The Empress of the fishpond
had asked for volunteers,
to go and fight the nasty thing
that filled them all with fear.
Perhaps you will remember
the very awful scene,
the nasty thing was leaking.
The fish were going green!

Two noble carp had offered
to see what was about
and now the rest had gathered
to wave their heroes out.
Kelpy Carp and Hi Lee
soon left them all behind
and headed towards the middle
to see what they could find.

Soon the pond grew darker,
the water was so still.
Everything was very quiet.
The heroes felt so ill.
"I think I see the nasty thing,"
Kelpy softly said.
"I see it too," said Hi Lee
"and the water's going red."

YUCKETYPOO

They edged a little closer
but soon they had to stop.
"What's that stink?"
gasped Hi Lee as he swam up to the top.
"Beats me, mate," said Kelpy.
"I'm feeling rather rough.
If we can't stop the nasty thing,
what will become of us?"

They swam a little closer.
Their eyes began to sting.
"I see it now!" cried Kelpy.
"I can see the dreadful thing!"

(Go to page 31)

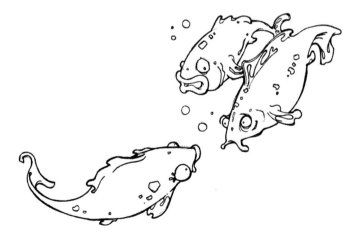

YUCKETYPOO

DUMPED

When the Dottos won the Lotto
one bright and sunny day,
they bought a lot of furniture
and sent the old away.
Two sofas though, were left behind,
and left out on the street.
They rotted till IT came along.

The monster now had feet!

YUCKETYPOO

THE WORSENING WHIFF

What a really rotten whiff!
It drifted in the air.
Folk held their breath and wouldn't sniff.
It really wasn't fair.
They travelled into London,
the Prime Minister to see.
They asked him "What's this horrid niff?"
He muttered "Don't ask me!"

YUCKETYPOO

THE LEFT BEHIND BROKEN TOYS

PART FOUR   "THE DOLL"

There once was a dolly named Peg
who was left when she broke off a leg.
Dropped in the road
she befriended a toad
and off they both hopped to be wed.

YUCKETYPOO

THE POND – PART FOUR

Something in the fishpond
had made the fish feel rough
as it sank below the water
and started leaking stuff.
Hi Lee Carp and Kelpy
didn't know what should be done.
Somehow they'd have to shift it
which wouldn't be much fun.

"We must attract attention,
before it is to late,"
said Kelpy Carp to Hi Lee
(who was in a dreadful state!)
They flip-flopped in the water,
gasping from the stink.
Along came the monster.

It wanted a drink.

(Go to page 36)

YUCKETYPOO

GROWING

TV in the flower bed.
Now the monster had a head.

Speakers moulding on the stairs.
Now the monster had some ears.

Broken china on the heath.
Now the monster had sharp teeth

Schoolbooks soggy by the drain.
Now the monster had a brain.

If only everybody knew,
how that monster grew and grew.

YUCKETYPOO

YUM YUM!

It rained all day
the rivers filled.
Onto the street,
the water spilled.
Dirty water,
very yucky,
catching rubbish,
very mucky.
Washing over
lots of streets.
Covering gardens,
soaking feet.
Leaving slime,
leaving sludge.
The monster thought it
looked like fudge!
Ate the lot,
filled its belly.
Made that monster

very smelly!

YUCKETYPOO

THE BIG CLEAN

The day dawned blue, the air was fresh,
the people gasped, there was no mess!
Every piece of rubbish gone!
They wondered what was going on?
No nasty niffs or pongy whiffs,
no plastic bags or cans.
Even the streams were nice and clean,
the people clapped their hands.
The pavements shone, the grass was green.
Everything was nice and clean.
"Perhaps," the people said aloud,
"the dustbin men have done us proud!"
"We've learned our lesson," people said,
"we like things nice and clean instead."
They danced and partied, tidied up,
left it neat without a fuss.
But soon they'd get a big surprise.
Now the monster was FULL SIZE!

YUCKETYPOO

SUMMER DAYS

For the next few days, they mended their ways
enjoying the town without a frown.
They sent a nice letter
for making things better.

The Prime Minister scratched his head.
"I don't get it, though," he said
as everyone cheered that the mess had been
cleared.
"I'll name today
NATIONAL NO RUBBISH DAY!"

Everyone had fun in the sun
"We like it clear! More ginger beer?"

YUCKETYPOO

THE POND – FINAL PART

The fish in the pond were astonished,
when, in the nick of time,
the nasty thing just vanished.
There was no trace of the slime.
Their human had come back from Brighton and
given the pond a good clean.
Kelpy and Hi Lee were happy. The pond was
the best it had been!

The Empress, however, was puzzled.
What was it that actually fell in?
If only she'd watched the monster,
swallow a rusty paint tin!
The monster had taken the rubbish and drank
all the slime clean away,
and now the Empress was smiling, as the fish
swam around all the day.

She thanked Kelpy Carp and Hi Lee
for being brave and bold,
threw a banquet in their honour –
and showered them with gold!

36

YUCKETYPOO

CREAKS, GROANS and VIBRATIONS

Something felt wrong
but no-one knew what,
the night was disturbed by the sound.
A creaking, groaning vibration
was coming from under the ground.
The houses rattled, the gardens shook.
Nobody knew what to do.
The pong came back and everyone yelled
"Oh no it's the Yucketypoo!"

YUCKETYPOO

THE YUCKETYPOO MONSTER

Out from under the ground it came,
huge and very smelly.
All it needed was one more thing –
a button for its belly.
People ran away in dread.
The monster stalked the street.
Built from all that rubbish,
from its head down to its feet.

It needed one more wrapper
to make it feel so strong.
Without a belly button,
something could go wrong.

"BRING ME A WRAPPER
AND I MEAN NOW!"
the monster rudely yelled.
"I'LL FALL TO BITS WITHOUT IT!"
It let off a horrible smell.

"Who can save us?" people said,
"Oh what are we to do?
It could be the end of our beautiful world,
all thanks to the Yucketypoo!"

YUCKETYPOO

THE PRIME MINISTER'S DECISION

The Prime Minister called a meeting
and everyone agreed,
that a law must pass
no rubbish be thrown,
the monster was in need.
"He'll fall apart," the Prime Minister said,
"if he can't get one last thing.
Give rubbish sacks to everyone
to put their rubbish in!"

YUCKETYPOO

The days and nights
went marching by,
the monster looked to see
if a single wrapper could be found
to make it strong and free.
But nothing could it find at all,
the Monster bellowed crossly.
Then Careless Annie came along
chewing on a toffee.
"Yum!" she said,
"I must have more!"
She opened up a sweet.
As everybody shouted "NO!!!"

she dropped it on the street.

YUCKETYPOO

THE MONSTER'S BELLY BUTTON

BOOM! BOOM! BOOM!
The monster appeared,
Annie let out a screech.
Lying between them on the ground
- the wrapper from her sweet!
"MY BELLY BUTTON!"
the monster roared.
"AT LAST IT HAS BEEN FOUND!"
It quickly went towards it,
stomping on the ground.
But as it bent to pick it up,
a holler filled the air.
Kym (remember her?) shouted out
"Who left that rubbish there!"
She placed the wrapper in the bin.
The monster stared in shock.
After a while, it let out a roar
and then it began to rock.

YUCKETYPOO

"SHE TOOK MY BELLY BUTTON!
AND NOW I'LL NEVER WIN!
SHE TOOK MY BELLY BUTTON
AND PUT IT IN THE BIN!"

It howled and hollered,
stamped its feet
then ran across the ground.
Roaring, screeching, yelling out,
making a terrible sound.
"You saved us, Kym!" Prime Minister said,
"Give that girl some gold!
The monster's gone! You did us proud.
You're really very bold!"

YUCKETYPOO

CELEBRATIONS

Kym was a hero.
Parties were held.
Celebrations galore.
No-one knew where
that monster had gone.
They didn't care any more.
"Three cheers for Kym!"
everyone said,
for Kym had saved the world.
"Hip hip hooray, hip hip hooray!
She is a clever girl!"

That's the end of our story
But now the whole world knows ...

YUCKETYPOO

… IF YOU THROW YOUR RUBBISH
ON THE GROUND,

THE MONSTER
GROWS

AND GROWS!

YUCKETYPOO.COM

FIND OUT MORE ABOUT THE
YUCKETYPOO MONSTER
AND HIS ADVENTURES

VISIT WWW.YUCKETYPOO.CO.UK

COMING SOON

YUCKETYPOO - SLIMES AGAIN
&
YUCKETYPOO - CLEANS UP

WRITTEN BY
JILLY HENDERSON-LONG

ILLUSTRATED BY
ASHLEY STEVENS

Lightning Source UK Ltd.
Milton Keynes UK
10 February 2010

149855UK00001B/80/P